Wanda
and the Alien
the Go
Camping

Sue Hendra

For our Wanda with love from Mummy and Daddy

WANDA AND THE ALIEN GO CAMPING

A RED FOX BOOK 978 1 849 41588 0

Published in Great Britain by Red Fox,

an imprint of Random House Children's Publishers UK

A Random House Group Company

This edition published 2014

1 3 5 7 9 10 8 6 4 2

Copyright © Paul Linnet and Sue Hendra, 2014

Red Fox Books are published by Random House Children's Publishers UK,

61–63 Uxbridge Road, London, W5 5SA

www.**randomhouse**.co.uk   www.**randomhousechildrens**.co.uk

Addresses for companies within The Random House Group Limited can be found at:

www.randomhouse.co.uk/offices.htm

THE RANDOM HOUSE GROUP Limited Reg. No. 954009

A CIP catalogue record for this book is available from the British Library

Printed in China

The Random House Group Limited supports the Forest Stewardship Council® (FSC®), the leading
international forest-certification organisation. Our books carrying the FSC label are printed on FSC®-certified paper.
FSC is the only forest-certification scheme supported by the leading environmental organisations, including Greenpeace.
Our paper procurement policy can be found at www.randomhouse.co.uk/environment

Wanda was all set to take her best friend,
the alien, on his very first camping trip,
but the weather was miserable.

They waited,

and waited

and waited.

Would it ever stop raining?

It was getting later and later.

"We'll just have to go camping another day," said Wanda sadly.

**Then, all of a sudden,
the alien had an idea!**

**He passed Wanda
her umbrella,**

**helped her on with
her backpack,**

**took her hand
and ran with her,
all the way...**

. . . to his rocket.

As they zoomed into space,
Wanda realized where they were going.
"Of course!" she said.
"We can camp on your planet!"

Wanda had been camping lots of times. She had come prepared. In her backpack she had packed . . .

**a mallet to bang
in the tent pegs,**

**a torch so they
could see at night,**

a bedtime story

**and some tasty snacks
to eat in the tent.**

The alien didn't really know what camping was.
So in his backpack he had packed . . .

his duck,

his cactus,

some balloons

and his rubber ring.

While they were in the rocket, Wanda tried
to show the alien how to put up the tent.

The alien had **a lot** to learn about camping.

As they flew, Wanda thought
of her favourite place to camp.
"We need to find somewhere
beautiful," she said.

Once they landed on the alien's planet,
the alien took Wanda's hand.

**They flew to the most beautiful place
he could think of . . .**

. . . the alien city. This wasn't quite what Wanda had in mind.

"It's a bit noisy here!" she shouted.

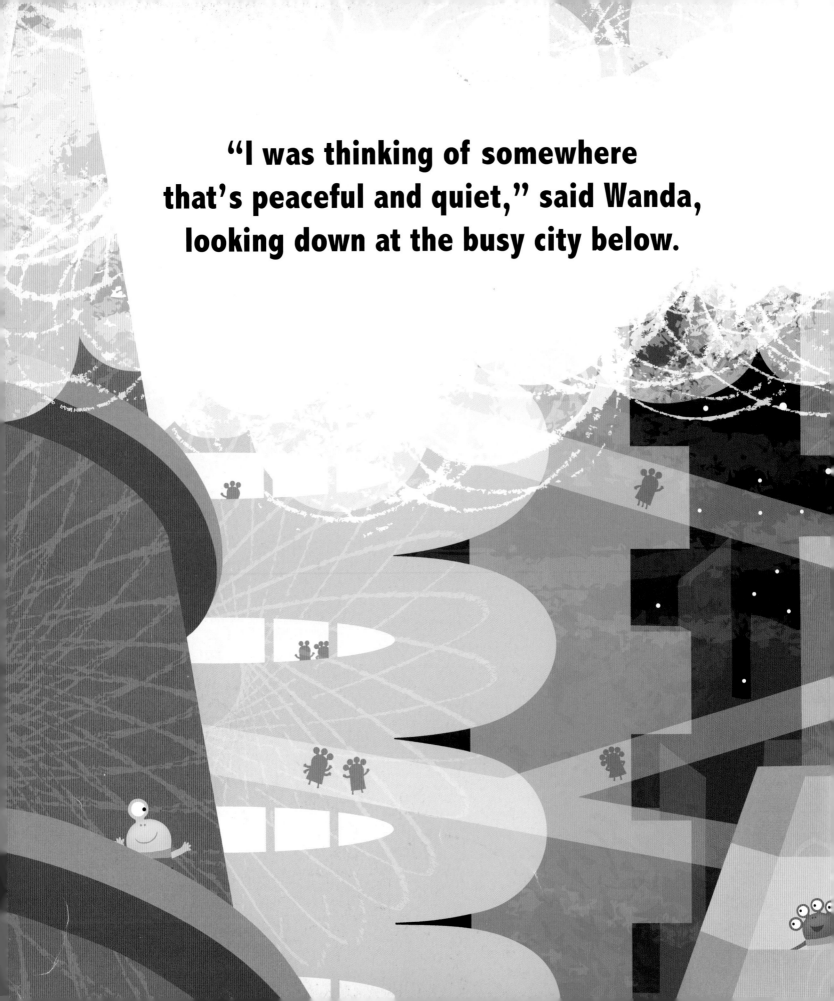

"I was thinking of somewhere
that's peaceful and quiet," said Wanda,
looking down at the busy city below.

Luckily the alien knew just the place . . .

but it was just a little bit *too* quiet . . .

Wanda didn't want to hurt the alien's
feelings, but these places weren't right.
"Maybe somewhere with wildlife
would be better?" she said.
The alien thought of somewhere
straight away . . .

**But the wildlife on the alien planet
was a bit *too* wild!**

"Perhaps there just isn't anywhere on your planet that's good for camping," said Wanda sadly. The alien nodded in agreement and Wanda looked even sadder.

**But then a smile started
to creep across the alien's face,
and he pointed up at the sky.**

They wouldn't camp **on** the alien planet, but up **above** it!

"Cloud camping," said Wanda.
"It's *perfect*! We can invite all your friends!
And one thing's for sure . . .

. . . it won't matter if it rains!"

So finally, side by side under
the stars, everything felt right.

"Now *this* is camping," said Wanda.